THE FAWN Animal Disg No Accounting For Tackets to the FAWN ARE COLDER

COLDER, No Accounting For

eepy Heads Going Places Tail Sleepy Hea

Don't Look Like Your Mother, THAT ARE COLDER

astes Animal Hou Bill Sleepy Hea

ackets Tail Twisters Filling the Bill Sleepy Hea "You Don't Look

Robin to the FAWN Animal Disguises "You Don't Look

No Accounting For Tastes A

DAYS ARE COLDER, No Accounting For Robin to

Places Animal Jackets

Bill Sleepy Heads Going Places Animal Jackets Robin to T

"You Don't Look Like Your Mother," Said the Robin to T DAYS ARE

s "You Don't Look Like Your Mother," Said the Robin to DAYS ARE

For Tastes Animal Houses Now That Days Are

Now That Days Are Filling the Bill Slee

Animal Jackets Tail Twisters Filling the Bill Slee "You Do

g For Tastes Animal Houses Now That Days Are Ta

Animal Jackets Tail Twisters Filling Animal Ta

Said the Robin to the FAWN Animal Disguises "You Accounting For Ta

No Accounting For Ta

OW THAT DAYS ARE COLDER, No Accounting Places Animal Ta

g the Bill Sleepy Heads Going Places Animal Said the R

Your Mother," Said the Now That

Animal Houses Now That

"You Don't Look Like Your Mother," Filling the

Tail Twisters

bowmar

Tail Twisters

by Aileen Fisher

designed and illustrated by Albert John Pucci · lettering by Paul Taylor

...to Ruth Gagliardo

I wonder why rabbits have tails
so small?

They aren't any good for wagging
at all

like tails  of dogs.

I wonder why rabbits have tails
so slight?
They aren't any good for blankets
at night

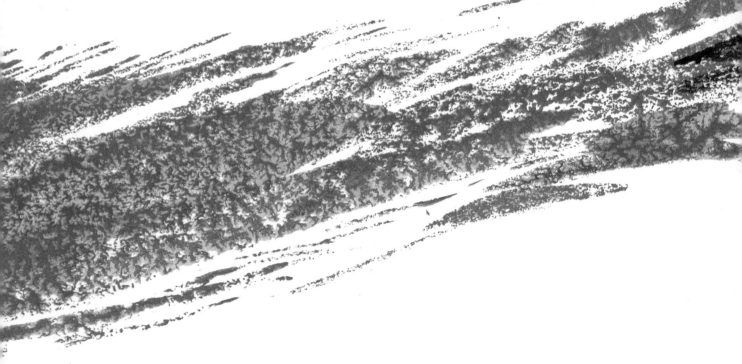

like tails of foxes.

And tails of rabbits in shape
and in size
aren't good for swatting
mosquitoes and flies

like tails that horses

and cattle prize.

I wonder why rabbits have tails
so soft?
They aren't any good for dangling
aloft

like tails of monkeys.

They aren't any good for rabbits
to use
as a stool to sit on

like kangaroos!

They aren't any good for striking
at foes,
like crocodile tails

with mighty BLOWS!

I wonder why rabbits have tails
so round?
They aren't any good for making
a sound
and giving a warning
when someone's around

like tails of beavers.

They aren't any good as rudders
to steer with
or use as propellers
to swim far and near with

like tails of fish.

I wonder why rabbits have tails

so short?

They aren't any good to use

as support

like woodpecker tails.

They aren't any good for feeling the way
when backing through tunnels
beneath the hay
like tails of gophers.

They aren't any good for beauty and show

like tails that peacocks
and roosters grow.

So why do rabbits grow tails
of fluff
as white underneath as a
powder puff?

What use
can the tail of a rabbit be?
There's only one thought
that occurs to me.

When a rabbit runs
from his many foes,

he raises his tail
     so the whiteness shows.

This catches the enemy's eye
with force,

as the rabbit speeds on his zigzag course.

Then
suddenly
PLUNK!
beside the trail,
the rabbit sits down
on his flashy tail.

And the enemy
doesn't know where to go,
the cottontail simply
doesn't show!

So often a rabbit is saved
that way
on his zigzag trail
through the woods and hay.

And squatting like that
is hard to beat

on such a soft and pillowy seat.

No Accounting For Tastes Going Places Animal Jackets "Said the Robin to the Fawn" Now That Days Are Colder Sleepy Heads Filling the Bill Tail Twisters Animal Houses Animal Disguises "You Don't Look Like Your Mother"